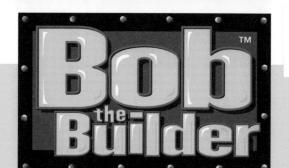

Bob the Builder™

Bob's Pizza

adapted by
Louisa Campbell

based on the script by
Ian Carney

SIMON SPOTLIGHT
New York　London　Toronto　Sydney

Based upon the television series *Bob the Builder*™ created by HIT Entertainment PLC
and Keith Chapman, as seen on Nick Jr.® Photos by HOT Animation.

SIMON SPOTLIGHT
An imprint of Simon & Schuster Children's Publishing Division
1230 Avenue of the Americas, New York, New York 10020

Manufactured in the United States of America

2 4 6 8 10 9 7 5 3 1

ISBN 0-689-86504-X

T 54650

Wendy had a big job for Roley and Muck. "Today we're going to build a lane just for bicycles on one of our town's busy roads," she said.

Spud came by the job site. He wanted to help. Mr. Bentley was happy to have help, so he handed Spud a walkie-talkie and a traffic sign.

Spud was excited! "Hello! This is Spud speaking," he said into the walkie-talkie, "and walking while I talk!"

"Okay, Spud," said Mr. Bentley, "stop any car that comes along, then call me and ask if the road is clear. If it is, you can let the cars through. Do you understand?"

Spud pretended he had been listening. "Ah, uh . . . yes, Mr. Bentley. Yes, of course I do. Spud's on the job!"

Down the street at Mr. Sabatini's Pizza, Scoop and Bob were on another job.

Mr. Sabatini explained, "My conveyor belt that carries the pizza through the oven won't work!"

"All right, I'll get to work!" said Bob.

Bob fixed the conveyor belt. But Mr. Sabatini was still unhappy. "The pizza is all burnt!" he said.

"Don't worry," said Bob. "I know what I need to do. I just have to speed up the conveyor belt!"

When Bob had fixed the speed of the conveyor belt, out came a perfect pizza. "It's a disaster!" said Mr. Sabatini.

Bob was confused. "But the pizza looks very nice," he said.

"The pizza is fabulous, Bob," said Mr. Sabatini. "The disaster is that my delivery man has called in sick! How am I going to deliver the pizzas?"

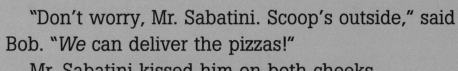

"Don't worry, Mr. Sabatini. Scoop's outside," said Bob. "*We* can deliver the pizzas!"

Mr. Sabatini kissed him on both cheeks. "*Magnifico,* Bob! You have saved the day!"

"I'll help you bake the pizzas too," said Bob. He threw a flat circle of dough high up into the air.

Plop! It landed right smack on top of Bob's head. It looked like a silly hat. Mr. Sabatini grinned. "I think you should just deliver the pizzas, Bob!"

Meanwhile Wendy and her team were working hard on the bicycle lane.

"Okay, Dizzy," she said, "start mixing the cement with this green dye. The path is green so cyclists will know that it's a safe place to ride."

Soon Bob and Scoop were delivering pizzas. They brought one to Mrs. Potts.

After they delivered a pizza to Mr. Dixon, there was just one pizza left in the scoop. "We'd better get it to Mr. Fothergill while it's still hot!" Bob said.

"No prob, Bob," Scoop said as he zoomed off.

There was a traffic jam up ahead.

"I'll go see what the problem is," said Bob. He saw Spud holding
up the red side of his traffic sign in front of Travis and Lofty.

"Spud's holding up traffic!" Travis exclaimed.

"Sorry, Travis," Spud said. "I can't let you go."

"You're supposed to use your walkie-talkie to ask Mr. Bentley if the road is clear," Bob told Spud.

Over the walkie-talkie Mr. Bentley said, "I've been wondering why there hasn't been any traffic all morning! The road is clear." Spud stepped aside to let everyone pass through.

Bob and Scoop finally made their last delivery. "Here's your pizza, Mr. Fothergill."

"Oh, it's not for me—sniff," said Mr. Fothergill. "I'm—sniff—allergic to pizza. It's for my—sniff—parrot, Hamish."

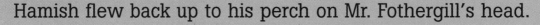

Mr. Fothergill flipped open the box, and Hamish swooped down and grabbed a bite. "Pizza parrot! Squawk! Pizza parrot!" he screeched.

Hamish flew back up to his perch on Mr. Fothergill's head.

Bob called Mr. Sabatini to let him know all the pizzas had been delivered.

"*Bellissimo,* Bob!" said Mr. Sabatini. "Now I will give you as much pizza as you can eat!"

"Thank you," said Bob. "Uh, you don't happen to have a pizza with apples or radishes or jam, do you?"

Wendy and her team were done with the bicycle lane. "All we need now," said Wendy, "is a bicycle to try it out." To everyone's surprise Mr. Bentley opened up his briefcase and pulled out and unfolded . . . a scooter!

"Very practical, Mr. Bentley," said Wendy, laughing as he swooshed away. "Bye!"

    Just then Bob and Scoop drove up. Scoop was carrying three
steaming pizzas. "I'm glad you're done, Wendy," said Bob, "because
we've brought lunch."

    "Oooh, Bob, that's great!" exclaimed Wendy.

    "Yes," continued Bob, handing out the pizzas, "a pineapple and corn
pizza for Wendy, a mushroom and onion deep-dish for me, and one
for Spud, too."

"Ah, my favorite!" Spud said as he took a slice. "It's the Spud Special—pizza with apple, radishes, *and* jam!"

DATE DUE

NOV 0 2 2009	APR 2 9 2013
DEC – 2 2009	SEP 0 4 2013
MAR 0 1 2010	APR 0 5 2014
SEP 0 1 2010	
SEP 14 2010	MAR 1 2 2015
OCT 1 8 2010	APR 3 0 2015
DEC 1 5 2010	JUN 0 5 2015
FEB 1 0 2011	AUG 1 2 2015
MAR 0 9 2011	OCT 0 7 2015
MAR 2 4 2011	FEB 2 6 2016
	MAY 1 9 2017
APR 2 1 2011	JUL 2 4 2017
SEP 1 5 2011	SEP 2 6 2017
APR 2 0 2012	
AUG 0 4 2012	JUL 1 4 2023
JAN 3 1 2013	
FEB 2 8 2013	